THE BIG BOOK
of
NURSERY TALES

STORIES IN THIS BOOK

Drakestail

The Fox and the Little Red Hen

The Ugly Duckling

Henny-Penny

The Gingerbread Boy

The Wolf and the Seven Little Kids

The Three Little Pigs

Goldilocks and The Three Bears

The Half-Chick

The Elves and The Shoemaker

Red Riding-Hood

The Three Billy Goats Gruff

THE BIG BOOK
of
NURSERY TALES

The Big Treasure Book of Nursery Tales

RETOLD BY Evelyn Andreas
PICTURES BY Leonard Weisgard

GROSSET & DUNLAP • Publishers
NEW YORK

ISBN: 0-448-04201-0
Copyright 1954 by Grosset & Dunlap, Inc.
Lithographed in the United States of America

1975 PRINTING

DRAKESTAIL

Drakestail was very little. That is why he was called Drakestail. But as little as he was, he was very smart and had more money than the king. The king had borrowed some of Drakestail's money, but never paid it back. So, one fine morning Drakestail set out for the palace.

"Quack, quack, quack, when shall I get my money back?" he sang to himself on the way. He looked so spruce and fresh that soon he made some friends. One was a Fox, one was a Ladder, one was a River, and one was a Wasp's Nest. They wanted to go along with him, so Drakestail tucked them all away in his pockets.

Soon Drakestail came to the king's palace. He marched up and asked to see the king. But the king knew what he wanted, so he planned to get rid of Drakestail.

He called his porter and said, "Throw him in with the turkeys and chickens." The turkeys and chickens jumped on Drakestail and began to peck him. But Drakestail called to his friend Fox,

"Reynard, Reynard, come out of your earth, Or Drakestail's life is of little worth!"

Friend Fox came out and—quick! quack! —all of the turkeys and chickens fled for their lives.

Then the king said, "Throw this tail of a drake into the well and make an end of him." But Drakestail called to his friend Ladder,

"Ladder, Ladder, come out of thy hold, Or Drakestail's days will soon be told!"

Out came friend Ladder, and Drakestail climbed up out of the well. Then the king became very angry.

"Throw him into the furnace!" said the king. At that moment Drakestail called out to his friend River,

"River, River, outward flow, Or to death Drakestail must go!"

The River came out, flooding the furnace, and all the soldiers besides. This made the king far more angry than ever. He roared, "Bring him to me! I'll take care of him!" When Drakestail was brought to the king, he saw the soldiers waiting, swords in hand. He called out to his last friend,

"Wasp's Nest, Wasp's Nest, make a sally, Or Drakestail nevermore will rally."

Out came the Wasps. They zoomed at the king and all his men. They stung so hard that all the soldiers and the king jumped out of the window and ran away.

Then Drakestail began to look for his money. He looked all over but he could not find it anywhere. At last he sat down on the king's throne to rest.

Meanwhile, the people came running. They couldn't find the king or his men, so they went into the palace to see what was happening. There was Drakestail sitting on the throne.

When the people saw him, they rejoiced and sang,

"The king is dead, long live the king! Heaven has sent us down this thing!"

And that is how Drakestail became king and lived happily ever after.

Once there was a little red hen who lived by herself in a house in the woods. A crafty old fox lived over the hill nearby. Every day he wondered how he could catch the little red hen to cook for his supper.

One day he put a bag over his shoulder and said to his mother, "Have the pot boiling when I come home, for I shall bring the little red hen for supper."

When he came to the house, he saw the little red hen outside gathering sticks for her fire. The fox slipped into the house. After a while, the hen went back into the house. When she saw the fox, she dropped her sticks and flew up to the rafters under the roof.

"I'll soon bring you down again," said the fox. He began to whirl around, faster and faster. This made the little red hen so dizzy that she fell down to the floor. Then the fox grabbed her and put her into his bag.

Over the hill and through the woods went the fox. After a while the fox got tired and he lay down to sleep for a while. Then the little red hen took out her scissors and snipped a hole in the bag.

THE FOX
and
THE LITTLE RED HEN

After she was out of the bag, the hen picked up a big stone, put it into the bag, and sewed up the hole. Then she ran home as fast as she could.

When the fox woke up, he started off again with the bag over his shoulder. The bag seemed to be much heavier.

"What a nice fat hen this is!" thought the fox. "And what a nice feast I shall have!"

When the fox got home, his mother was waiting at the door of the cave.

"Mother, have you got the pot boiling?" asked the fox.

"Yes, to be sure," said the mother. "And do you have the little red hen?"

"Right here in my bag," said the fox. "Lift up the lid of the pot, and I will throw her in."

The mother lifted the lid of the pot. The fox untied the bag and held it over the boiling water. But instead of the hen, the heavy stone fell into the water.

This made the fox and his mother feel so foolish that they let the little red hen alone after that, and so she lived safely and happily in her house in the woods for the rest of her life.

THE UGLY DUCKLING

One midsummer day a mother duck hatched her eggs. "Cheep, cheep," said the little ducklings as they poked their pretty heads out of their shells. But one big egg took much longer to hatch. When the shell broke open at last, a big and ugly duckling popped out. Everybody said he was ugly, even his own mother.

The poor little duckling was very unhappy in the farmyard. He was driven about by everyone. The ducks pecked at him. The chickens flapped their wings at him. Even the girl who fed the poultry kicked him. One day he decided to run away.

The little duckling walked and walked until he came to a big marsh where the wild ducks lived. He was so tired and miserable that he went to sleep in the rushes. In the morning he found the wild ducks staring at him.

"What sort of a duck are you?" they asked. "You are very ugly," they told him, and went away. Just then some hunters came along and began to shoot at the wild ducks and geese. "Bang! bang!" went the guns.

The wild ducks flew up into the air, but the ugly duckling went deeper into the rushes.

The hunting dogs ran into the marsh. One of them saw the ugly duckling and sniffed at him. Then he ran on. The duckling thought, "I am so ugly that even a dog won't bite me, but I guess that is something to be thankful for."

Then the duckling left the marsh and went on to find a new place to live. He walked and walked until he came to a little cottage. An old woman lived in the cottage with her cat and her hen. It was nighttime, and they were all asleep, so the duckling slipped inside to get some rest.

In the morning they found their visitor. The old woman could not see very well, so she thought it was a fat duck. "Fine!" she said. "Now we will have some duck's eggs." She let the duckling stay there.

But weeks went by and still there were no eggs. One day the hen said, "Can you lay eggs, like me?" The duckling said, "No." The hen said, "Then please keep quiet." The cat said, "Can you arch your back or purr?" The duckling said, "No." The cat said, "Then have the goodness to keep quiet." So the duckling sat all alone in a corner and kept quiet.

One day the duckling had a great longing to go for a swim. He told the hen and the cat about it. "What a foolish idea!" they both said. "*We* never go for a swim!" But still the duckling wanted to go, so he left the cottage.

It was autumn when the duckling found a lake. He stayed there so that he could swim every day. Soon the sky was wintry and the clouds hung heavy with snow. One evening a flock of beautiful birds appeared out of the bushes. They were pure white, with long graceful necks. They uttered a strange cry, spread their wings, and flew far away to a warmer land.

The ugly duckling had never seen such beautiful birds. He did not know that they were swans. But the sight of them gave him a strange feeling. Craning his neck, he uttered a little shriek. Although he could not fly after them, the duckling did not forget the lovely birds.

Winter came and it was bitterly cold. Soon the lake froze and there was no place for the duckling to swim. The poor little duckling suffered all through that long, hard winter.

After a time spring came again. The sun shone and the trees began to blossom. The ice melted and the little duckling could swim again. One day he flapped his wings and to his great surprise he found that he could fly. He flew into a big garden where the grass was green and the lilacs bloomed.

There, in front of him, on a little pond he saw three beautiful white swans. A strange feeling of sadness swept over him. "These are royal birds," he said. "I will fly to them. Perhaps they will kill me because I am so ugly. But that is better than being so lonely and unhappy."

He flew into the water and began to swim toward the birds. The stately birds saw him, ruffled their feathers, and started toward him. The duckling bent his head, thinking that they would kill him. But suddenly he saw his image reflected in the water below. And what did he see?

No longer was he an ugly dark gray bird. He was pure white like the others. The ugly duckling had grown up to be a beautiful swan! He lifted his head and saw the other swans swimming around him, stroking him with their bills. How happy he was!

Just then some children came into the garden with bread for the swans. "Oh! There is a new swan," they cried with joy. "And he is the most beautiful of them all!"

One day Henny-Penny was picking up corn in the farmyard when — whack! — something hit her upon the head. "Goodness gracious me!" said Henny-Penny, "the sky's a-falling. I must go and tell the king!"

So she went along and went along, until she met Cocky-Locky.

"Where are you going?" said Cocky-Locky.

"Oh, I'm going to tell the king the sky's a-falling," said Henny-Penny.

"May I come with you?" said Cocky-Locky.

"Certainly," said Henny-Penny.

So they went along and went along, until they met Ducky-Daddles. "Where are you going?" said Ducky-Daddles. "We're going to tell the king the sky's a-falling," said Henny-Penny and Cocky-Locky. "May I come with you?" said Ducky-Daddles. "Certainly," said they. So they all went along to tell the king the sky was a-falling.

They went along and went along, until they met Goosey-Poosey. "Where are you going?" said Goosey-Poosey. "We're going to tell the king the sky's a-falling," said Henny-Penny, Cocky-Locky and Ducky-Daddles. "May I go with you?" said Goosey-Poosey. "Certainly," said they. So they all went along to tell the king the sky was a-falling.

They went along and went along until they met Turkey-Lurkey. "Where are you going?" said Turkey-Lurkey. "We're going to tell the king the sky's a-falling," said Henny-Penny, Cocky-Locky, Ducky-Daddles and Goosey-Poosey. "May I go with you?" said Turkey-Lurkey. "Certainly," said they. So they all went along to tell the King the sky was a-falling.

They went along and went along and went along, until they met Foxy-Woxy. "Where are you going, Henny-Penny, Cocky-Locky, Ducky-Daddles, Goosey-Poosey and Turkey-Lurkey?" said Foxy-Woxy. "We're going to tell the king the sky's a-falling," said Henny-Penny, Cocky-Locky, Ducky-Dad-

dles, Goosey-Poosey and Turkey-Lurkey.

"Oh!" said Foxy-Woxy. "But that is not the way to the king. I know the proper way to the king's palace. Shall I show it to you?" "Certainly!" said Henny-Penny, Cocky-Locky, Ducky-Daddles, Goosey-Poosey and Turkey-Lurkey. So they all went along after Foxy-Woxy to the king's palace.

They went along and went along and went along until they came to a narrow and dark hole. This was the door to Foxy-Woxy's cave. But Foxy-Woxy said, "This is a short way to the king's palace. You will get there sooner if you follow me. I will go first, and you come after me."

"Why, of course, certainly, without doubt, why not?" said Henny-Penny, Cocky-Locky, Ducky-Daddles, Goosey-Poosey and Turkey-Lurkey.

So Foxy-Woxy went into his cave. He didn't go very far, but turned around to wait for Henny-Penny, Cocky-Locky, Ducky-Daddles, Goosey-Poosey and Turkey-Lur-key.

Turkey-Lurkey was the first to go into the dark hole. He had not gone far when — "Hrumph!" — he was quickly pounced upon and gobbled up by Foxy-Woxy.

Then Goosey-Poosey went in. And — "Hrumph!" — she, too, was gobbled up.

Now it was Ducky-Daddles' turn. He went waddling in, only to be gobbled up like the others.

Next, Cocky-Locky strutted in. And — "Hrumph!"

But Cocky-Locky *will* always crow, whether you want him to or not, and he had time for one big

"Cock-a-doodle-doo!"

before Henny-Penny could enter the cave.

When Henny-Penny heard Cocky-Locky crow, she said to herself, "My goodness! It must be dawn. Time for me to lay my egg!" So she turned right around and bustled off to her nest.

And she never told the king that the sky was a-falling!

THE GINGERBREAD BOY

Once there was a little old man and a little old woman. They lived in a little old house in the wood. One day the little old woman was baking gingerbread. She cut a cake in the shape of a boy, and put it into the oven.

Later, when she opened the oven door, out popped the little gingerbread boy. He began to run away as fast as he could go.

The little old woman and the little old man ran after him. But they could not catch him. The gingerbread boy ran on until he came to a barn full of threshers. He called out to them,

"I've run away from a little old woman,
 And a little old man,
And I can run away from you, I can!"

The threshers ran after the gingerbread boy. But they could not catch him. He ran on until he came to a field full of mowers. He called out,

"I've run away from a little old woman,
 A little old man,
 A barn full of threshers,
And I can run away from you, I can!"

Then the mowers ran after him. But they could not catch him. The gingerbread boy

ran on until he came to a cow. He called out,
"I've run away from a little old woman,
A little old man,
A barn full of threshers,
A field full of mowers,
And I can run away from you, I can!"
Then the cow ran after him. But she could not catch him. The gingerbread boy ran on until he came to a fox. He called out,
"I've run away from a little old woman,
A little old man,
A barn full of threshers,
A field full of mowers,
A cow,
And I can run away from you, I can!"

Then the fox ran after him. Now foxes can run very fast. So the fox caught him, and began to eat him up.

The gingerbread boy said, "Oh, dear! I'm quarter gone." Then he said, "Now I'm half gone!" Then he said, "Now I'm three-quarters gone!" At last he said, "Now I'm all gone!" And that was the end of the gingerbread boy.

The wolf and the seven little kids

A mother goat had seven little kids. One day she said to them, "I am going into the forest to get food. You must be on guard against the wolf. He will try to disguise himself to fool you, but you will know him by his rough voice and his black feet." Then the mother goat went into the forest.

Soon the seven little kids heard a knock on the door. A voice cried, "Open the door, dear little children, this is your mother. I have brought something nice for you to eat."

The kids heard the rough voice and knew it was the wolf. They said, "You are not our mother, for your voice is rough. You are the wolf!"

The wolf went away. He bought some chalk and ate it to make his voice soft. Then he went back to the house and knocked on the door. "Open the door, dear little children, this is your mother," he said.

But the wolf had laid his black paws against the window and the kids saw them. They said, "You are not our mother, for you have black feet. You are the wolf!"

The wolf went away again. He bought some dough from the baker and rubbed it on his feet. Then he sprinkled flour over the dough to make his feet white. Once more he went back to the house.

"Open the door, dear little children, this is your mother," he said. He put his white paws against the window. When the kids saw the white paws, they believed he was really their mother. They opened the door — and in sprang the wolf.

The poor little kids were terrified. They flew in all directions to hide. One went under the table. The second went into the bed.

The third hid in the stove. The fourth went into the kitchen. The fifth went into the cupboard. The sixth hid under the washbowl. The seventh and last kid scrambled up into the clock case.

But the wolf went after them all. One after the other, he gobbled up six little kids. But he could not find the seventh little kid who was hidden in the clock case. Then the wolf went off to the meadow to take a nap.

When the mother goat came home she could not find a single kid. Suddenly she heard a little voice from the clock case say, "Mother, mother, I am up here!" She took the kid out of the clock case, and he told her about the wolf.

They went out to the meadow and there they found the wolf asleep under a tree. The mother goat plucked a leaf from a bush and quickly used it to tickle the end of the goat's nose. Achoo! Achoo! One after another, out came all six little kids.

The wolf woke up. There before him were the six little kids he had just eaten! He could not believe his eyes. He jumped up in a terrible fright and ran off, never to be seen again.

After that, the mother goat and her seven little kids lived happily.

THE THREE LITTLE PIGS

Three little pigs went out to seek their fortunes. The first pig built himself a house of straw. Along came a wolf, who said, "Little pig, little pig, let me come in."

But the pig said, "No, by the hair of my chinny-chin-chin."

The wolf said, "I'll huff and I'll puff, and I'll blow your house in." He huffed and he puffed and he blew the house in. And the first little pig ran away.

The second pig built himself a house of sticks. Along came the wolf and said, "Little pig, little pig, let me come in."

But the pig said, "No, by the hair of my chinny-chin-chin."

The wolf said, "I'll huff and I'll puff, and I'll blow your house in." He huffed and he puffed, and he blew the house in. And the second little pig ran away.

The third pig built himself a house of bricks. Along came the wolf and said, "Little pig, little pig, let me come in."

But the pig said, "No, by the hair of my chinny-chin-chin."

The wolf said, "I'll huff and I'll puff, and I'll blow your house in." He huffed and he puffed, and he puffed and he huffed. But he could not blow the brick house down. Then he tried to coax the pig out of the house.

"Little pig, I know where there is a nice field of turnips," said the wolf. "I will call for you tomorrow and we will go to the turnip field together."

But the little pig was smart. Very early in the morning he went to the turnip field by himself. When the wolf called for him, he was back home. "I have my turnips already," he said, "and my dinner is all cooked."

The wolf thought up another trick. "Little pig, I know where there is a nice apple orchard," he said. "I shall take you there tomorrow." But the next day when the wolf came, the pig was gone.

The wolf ran over to the apple orchard, and there he saw the pig in one of the trees. "Why didn't you wait for me, little pig?" he said. "Are the apples good?"

. "Yes," said the pig, "they are very good apples. If you will stand over there, I will throw one down to you." The pig threw the apple as far as he could. While the wolf ran to get it, he jumped down and hurried home.

Then the wolf became very angry. He said he *would* get the little pig. He went up on the roof of the little pig's house and started to climb down the chimney.

But the smart little pig put a pot of water on the fire. The wolf came down the chimney and fell *kersplash!* into the water. He climbed out, very wet, and ran off.

So the three little pigs lived safely together in the little brick house ever after.

Goldilocks And The Three Bears

Once there were three Bears who lived in a little house in the woods. The father was Great Big Bear. The mother was Middle-sized Bear, and the child was Teeny-Tiny Bear. One day, while their porridge was cooling off, they went for a walk.

Along came a little girl named Goldilocks. She knocked at the door but no one answered. She walked in and there she saw the three bowls of porridge on the table. "I am very hungry," thought Goldilocks.

First she tasted the porridge in the great big bowl but it was too hot. Then she tasted the porridge in the middle-sized bowl but it was too cool. Then she tasted the porridge in the teeny-tiny bowl and it was just right. So she ate it all up.

After that Goldilocks went into another room. And there she saw three chairs. First she sat down in the great big chair but it was too high. Then she sat down in the middle-sized chair but it was too low. When she sat down in the teeny-tiny chair, she said, "This is just right!" And Goldilocks sat down so hard that the bottom of the chair fell to the floor.

After that Goldilocks went up to the bedroom. And there she saw three beds. First she tried the great big bed but it was too hard. Then she tried the middle-sized bed but it was too soft. But when she lay down on the teeny-tiny bed, it was just right. Goldilocks fell fast asleep.

While she was sleeping, the three Bears returned from their walk. They looked at the table.

"SOMEONE HAS BEEN TASTING MY PORRIDGE," said the Great Big Bear in a great big voice.

"SOMEONE HAS BEEN TASTING MY PORRIDGE," said the Middle-sized Bear in a middle-sized voice.

"*Someone has been tasting my porridge and has eaten it all up!*" said the Teeny-Tiny Bear in a teeny-tiny voice.

Then the three Bears went into the next room, which was the parlor.

"SOMEONE HAS BEEN SITTING IN MY CHAIR," said the Great Big Bear in his great big voice.

"SOMEONE HAS BEEN SITTING IN MY CHAIR," said the Middle-sized Bear in a middle-sized voice.

"*Someone has been sitting in my chair, and it is all broken,*" said the Teeny-Tiny Bear in a teeny-tiny voice.

Then the three Bears went upstairs to the bedroom.

"SOMEONE HAS BEEN LYING IN MY BED," said the Great Big Bear in his great big voice.

"SOMEONE HAS BEEN LYING IN MY BED," said the Middle-sized Bear in a middle-sized voice.

"*Someone has been lying in my bed — and here she is!*" said the Teeny-Tiny Bear in a teeny-tiny voice.

The voices woke up Goldilocks. When she saw the three Bears staring at her, she jumped out of the window, and luckily landed in a pile of soft leaves. Then she ran home as fast as her legs would carry her.

THE HALF-CHICK

Once there was a chicken who was really only half a chicken. He was named Medio Pollito, which is Spanish for half-chick. This half-chick was very naughty and one day he ran away from home to see the king at Madrid. Hoppity-kick, hoppity-kick, off he stumped toward Madrid.

On the way he came to a Stream that was all choked up with weeds. The Stream said to Medio Pollito, "Please help me and clear away the weeds so that I can flow again." But Medio Pollito said, "No, I have more important things to do," and went on his way.

Then he came to a Fire that was burning very low. "Please put some sticks on me so that I will not die out," said the Fire. But Medio Pollito said, "No, I have more important things to do," and went on his way.

Then he came to the Wind who was tangled up in the branches of a tree. "Please help me get untangled," said the Wind. But Medio Pollito said, "No, I can't waste my time on such trifles. I have more important things to do."

After a while Medio Pollito came to Madrid. He stumped up to the king's palace. But as he was hopping past one of the back windows, the king's cook saw him.

"Now, that's just what I need for the king's dinner," said the cook. He reached out and grabbed Medio Pollito. Then he popped the half-chick into the broth pot standing on the fire.

"Oh, Water, Water," cried Medio Pollito, "have pity on me and do not wet me like this!" But the Water replied, "You would not help me when I was a Stream choked with weeds. Now you must be punished."

When the fire began to heat the water, Medio Pollito cried out, "Fire, Fire, don't scorch me like this!" But the Fire replied, "You would not help me when I was dying out in the wood. Now you must be punished."

At that moment the cook looked into the pot and saw Medio Pollito jumping around, all wet and scorched. "This is no good for the king's dinner," he said. And he threw the half-chick out of the window. The Wind caught him up and whirled him in the air.

"Oh, Wind," cried Medio Pollito, "I am so tired—do let me rest a moment!" But the Wind said, "You would not help me when I was tangled up in the tree. Now you must be punished."

The Wind whirled him higher and higher and higher — up to the highest steeple of the Church. There the Wind fastened Medio Pollito. And there the half-chick stands to this very day.

THE ELVES
AND THE SHOEMAKER

One day a poor shoemaker found that he had only enough leather left for one pair of shoes. He cut them out one evening before he went to bed, thinking that he would finish them the next day.

The next day, after breakfast, the shoemaker went to his work table. And there he saw the shoes all finished and ready to wear. He called his wife and they both stared in amazement. They could not imagine who had finished the shoes.

That same day a customer bought the shoes. They were so well made that he was glad to pay a good price for them. Now the shoemaker had enough money to buy leather for two pairs of shoes.

That evening he again cut out the shoes, thinking to work on them the next day. But the next day he found the shoes all finished and ready to wear. Two customers came in and bought both pairs of shoes. They said, "What fine stitches! How well made they are!" Now the shoemaker could buy leather for four pairs of shoes.

This went on for some time. Each night the shoemaker would cut out the leather.

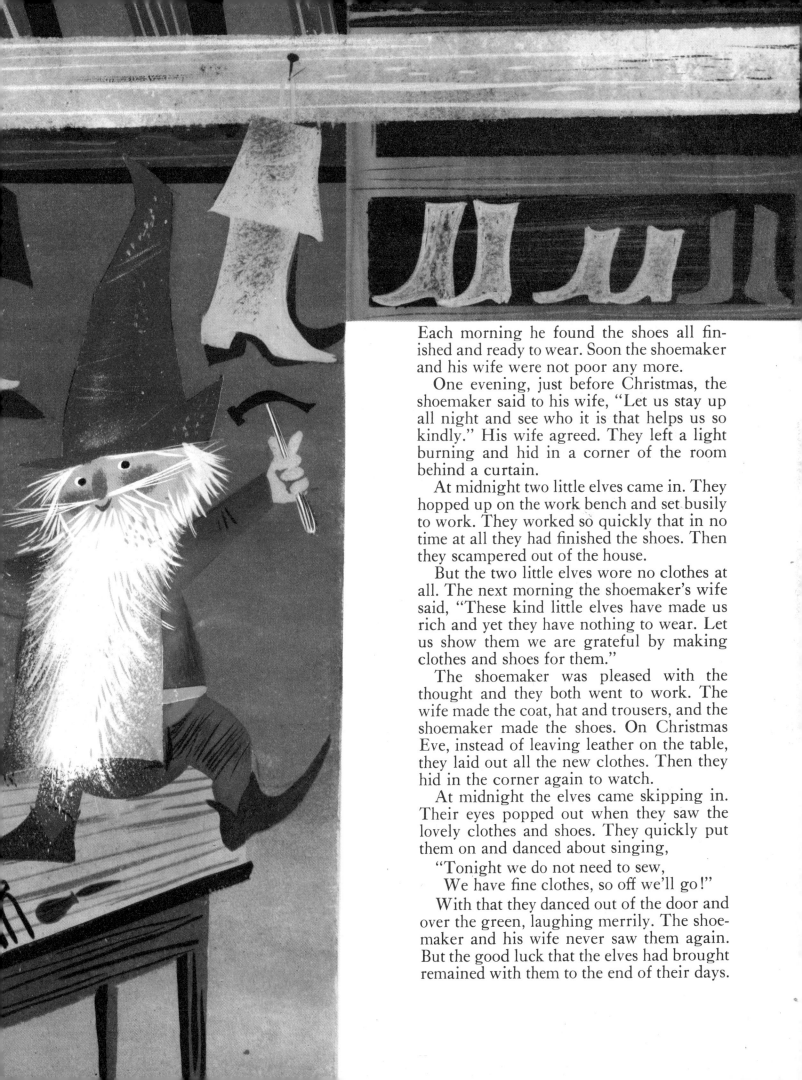

Each morning he found the shoes all finished and ready to wear. Soon the shoemaker and his wife were not poor any more.

One evening, just before Christmas, the shoemaker said to his wife, "Let us stay up all night and see who it is that helps us so kindly." His wife agreed. They left a light burning and hid in a corner of the room behind a curtain.

At midnight two little elves came in. They hopped up on the work bench and set busily to work. They worked so quickly that in no time at all they had finished the shoes. Then they scampered out of the house.

But the two little elves wore no clothes at all. The next morning the shoemaker's wife said, "These kind little elves have made us rich and yet they have nothing to wear. Let us show them we are grateful by making clothes and shoes for them."

The shoemaker was pleased with the thought and they both went to work. The wife made the coat, hat and trousers, and the shoemaker made the shoes. On Christmas Eve, instead of leaving leather on the table, they laid out all the new clothes. Then they hid in the corner again to watch.

At midnight the elves came skipping in. Their eyes popped out when they saw the lovely clothes and shoes. They quickly put them on and danced about singing,

"Tonight we do not need to sew,
 We have fine clothes, so off we'll go!"

With that they danced out of the door and over the green, laughing merrily. The shoemaker and his wife never saw them again. But the good luck that the elves had brought remained with them to the end of their days.

RED RIDING-HOOD

Once there was a little girl who wore a red cloak and hood, and so she was called Red Riding-Hood. One day her mother gave her a basket of cakes to take to her grandmother who lived in the wood.

On the way she met a wolf. He said, "Where are you going, Red Riding-Hood?" She told him that she was going to her grandmother's house. Then, while Red Riding-Hood stopped to pick some flowers, the wolf ran ahead to the grandmother's house. He knocked on the door.

"Who is there?" asked the grandmother from her bed.

"This is little Red Riding-Hood," said the wolf, speaking in a soft voice.

"Press the latch and come in," said the grandmother. But when she saw the wolf come in, she jumped out of bed and hid in the closet.

The wolf put on the grandmother's night-cap and crawled under the covers. Pretty soon, he heard a knock on the door.

"Who is there?" asked the wolf in a very soft voice.

"This is Red Riding-Hood," said the girl.

"Press the latch and come in," said the wolf. Red Riding-Hood went in and stood near the bed. She thought her grandmother looked strange.

"Oh, Grandmother, what big ears you have!" said Red Riding-Hood.

"The better to hear you with, my dear," said the wolf.

"Oh, Grandmother, what big eyes you have!" said Red Riding-Hood.

"The better to see you with, my dear," said the wolf.

"But Grandmother, what big teeth you have!" said Red Riding-Hood.

"The better to eat you with, my dear!" said the wolf, and with that he sprang out of bed.

Luckily, at that very moment a hunter was passing by. Hearing Red Riding Hood's screams, he rushed in. But the wolf saw the hunter coming and he jumped out the window and ran away, never to return.

The grandmother came out of the closet and thanked the hunter. Then they all sat down to have tea and cakes.

THE THREE BILLY GOATS GRUFF

Once there were three Billy Goats named Gruff. They had to cross a bridge to get to their food. Under the bridge lived a Troll who had a long nose and eyes like saucers.

First the youngest Billy Goat Gruff started to cross the bridge. "Trip, trap, trip, trap!" went the bridge.

"*Who's that tripping over my bridge?*" roared the Troll.

"It is I," said the youngest Billy Goat Gruff in a tiny voice.

"I am coming to gobble you up!" said the Troll. But the youngest Billy Goat Gruff said, "I'm too small. Why don't you wait for my brother who is bigger?" So the Troll let him go.

Then the second Billy Goat Gruff started to cross the bridge. "Trip, trap, trip, trap!" went the bridge.

"*Who's that tripping over my bridge?*" roared the Troll.

"It is I," said the second Billy Goat Gruff in a middle-sized voice.

"I am coming to gobble you up!" said the Troll. But the second Billy Goat Gruff said, "Why don't you wait for my brother who is bigger?" So the Troll let him go.

Then came the big Billy Goat Gruff. "Trip, trap, trip, trap!" went the bridge, groaning because he was so heavy."

"*Who's that tramping over my bridge?*" roared the Troll.

"It is I," said the Billy Goat Gruff in a great big voice.

"I am coming to gobble you up!" said the Troll. But the big Billy Goat Gruff had two big strong horns. When the Troll came up, he lowered his head and butted the Troll right into the river.

And that was the end of the Troll. So —
Snip, snap, snout,
This tale's told out.